The Haunted House

by Joy Cowley

I am a ghostie,
a big scary ghostie.

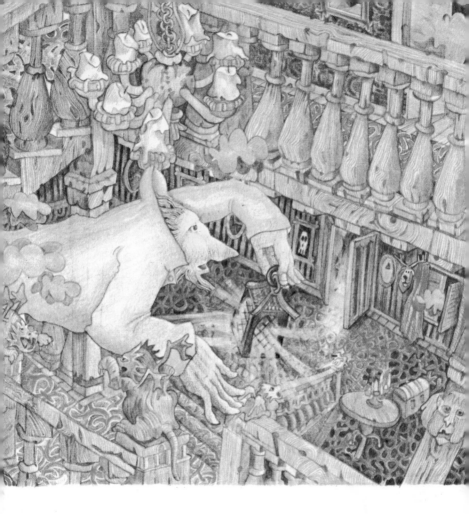

I live in the haunted house,
and I go...

I am a spook owl,
a big scary spook owl.

6

I live in the haunted house,
and I go...

I am a monster,
a big scary monster.

10

I live in the haunted house,
and I go...

I am Antonio,
a little boy, Antonio.

I am in the haunted house,

and I'm not scared of **you.**

Shoo! Shoo! Shoo!